Princess Pig
and Marvin

Written by Michèle Dufresne
Illustrated by Ann Caranci

PIONEER VALLEY EDUCATIONAL PRESS, INC.

Here is Princess.
Princess is a pig.

Look at Marvin.
Marvin is a pig, too.

5

Princess and Marvin
like to play in the water.

Princess and Marvin
like to swing.

Princess and Marvin
like to jump.

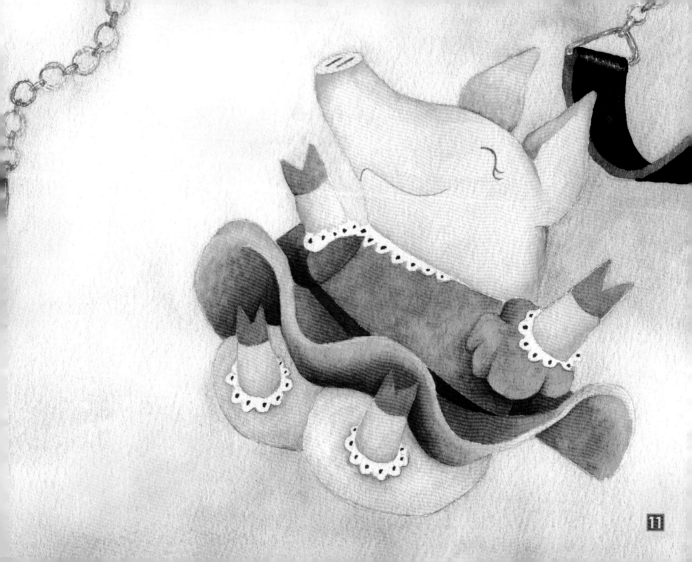

Princess and Marvin
like to jump into the mud.